RIDING FREE

Meet the PALS

EGMONT
We bring stories to life

First published in 2020 in the USA by Little, Brown and Company.
This edition published in Great Britain in 2021 by Egmont Books

An imprint of HarperCollins*Publisher*s
1 London Bridge Street.
London SE1 9GF

www.egmontbooks.co.uk

ISBN 978 0 7555 0116 8

71367/001

Printed in Singapore

Meet the PALS

Attention, DreamWorks Spirit Riding Free fans!

Look for these words when you read
this book. Can you spot them all?

home

friends

ride

horse

Reading Together

Before you start reading, it helps to talk about
what you think the book might be about.

Does the title help you?
Are there any clues on the cover?

Sound out unfamiliar words and look for clues in
the pictures. Sometimes the words before and after
an unknown word can help work out what
a difficult word means.

After you've finished the story, go back to any words
that you found tricky and talk about what they mean.
This helps you to remember them!

Activities for after reading

Can you spot these words in the story?

ranch   **believes**   **Spirit**   **special**

What does each word mean? How do you know?

Question Time!

Why did Lucky find it hard to make friends
at her new school?

How would you feel starting at a new school?

Advanced Question

What is the difference between a wild animal and a pet?

Meet Lucky.

She is moving from a big city

to a small town named Miradero.

Lucky

Lucky goes on a train to town.

Will she like her new home?

Lucky goes to school.

It is her first day.

She wears her best dress.

The other kids give her funny looks.

Being new is hard.

Lucky has no friends yet.

She eats lunch alone.

Soon Lucky makes new friends.
'I am Pru,' a girl says.

Pru

"And I am Abigail.
Do you want to come
riding with us?"

Abigail

Pru's dad has a horse ranch.

Pru and Abigail are great riders.

Pru's horse is named
Chica Linda.

Abigail's horse is named
Boomerang.

Lucky likes horses,

but she does not know how to ride.

Lucky meets a horse named Spirit.

Spirit is wild.

No one can ride him.

Lucky knows Spirit is special.

"Hey there," she says gently.

Spirit likes Lucky, too.

Spirit lets Lucky ride him.

"Whoa, boy!" she says.

"Slow down!"

Lucky can ride with Pru and Abigail!

Later, Pru's dad says,

"Lucky, Spirit should be yours.

No one else can ride him."

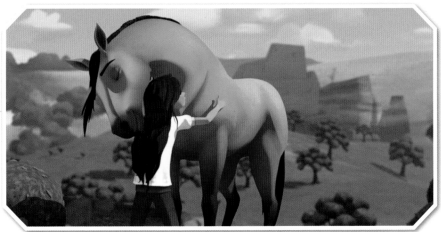

Lucky loves Spirit,

but she cannot keep him.

She believes no one can own Spirit

because he is wild at heart.

So Lucky lets Spirit go.

"Goodbye, Spirit.

Be free," says Lucky.

Spirit runs through the hills.

But he is not gone for long!
Spirit loves Lucky and
comes back to her.

Lucky and Spirit can keep riding with Lucky's new friends. Together, **P**ru, **A**bigail and **L**ucky are the **PAL**s.

Their horses Chica Linda,
Boomerang and Spirit
are pals, too.

"Come on, PALs!" Lucky calls.

These friends are always ready to ride off on an adventure.

Now Miradero feels like home.

There is no place
Lucky would rather be.

Lucky loves being here
with Spirit, riding free!